MW00995431

To Gio, Ivry, Eli, and Levi:
As your dads, we are endlessly proud of the incredible individuals
you are becoming. This book is for you, with all our love.
—J.W. and A.G.

Paloma and Liliana,
the love that this dad has for you both is beyond measure.
—D.E.C.

Visit us on the Web! rhcbooks.com

Educators and librarians, for a variety of teaching tools, visit us at RHTeachersLibrarians.com

Library of Congress Cataloging-in-Publication Data is available upon request.
ISBN 978-0-593-57216-0 (trade) — ISBN 978-0-593-57217-7 (lib. bdg.) — ISBN 978-0-593-57218-4 (ebook)

The artist used digital media to create the illustrations for this book.
The text of this book is set in 16-point Grota Rounded.
Interior design by Elizabeth Tardiff

MANUFACTURED IN CHINA
10 9 8 7 6 5 4 3 2 1
First Edition

Love, Dad

Inspiring Notes from Fathers to Kids

by Dr. Joel Warsh & Andrew Gardner

illustrated by David Elmo Cooper

Random House New York

Dear Kiddo,

To make this very special book for you, we went to lots of dads and asked them what they hoped to teach their kids, what lessons they wanted to pass on, what wishes they had for their kids' lives. It is full of those hopes and dreams for your future, those messages of guidance and words of wisdom that you can keep with you always.

When you grow up,
I hope you . . .

. . . don't let the world change your smile.
Instead, let your smile change the world.

I hope you shine a rainbow

from your heart for all the world to see.

I hope you believe that superheroes exist
in all colors, shapes, sizes, and genders—
and that most of them don't wear capes.

I hope you love your life and
treasure every season along the way.

I hope you always remember to choose
happiness and the things that make you laugh.

I hope you love big—
and I hope the biggest love you have is for yourself.

I hope you know there is always
something to be thankful for.

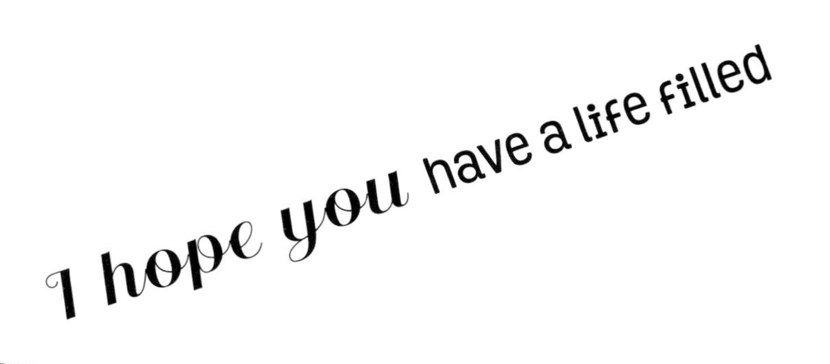

I hope you have a life filled

with dreams that come true!

I hope you feel love in every cell of your body,
a boundless love that fills every day with happiness
and circulates back into the world around you.

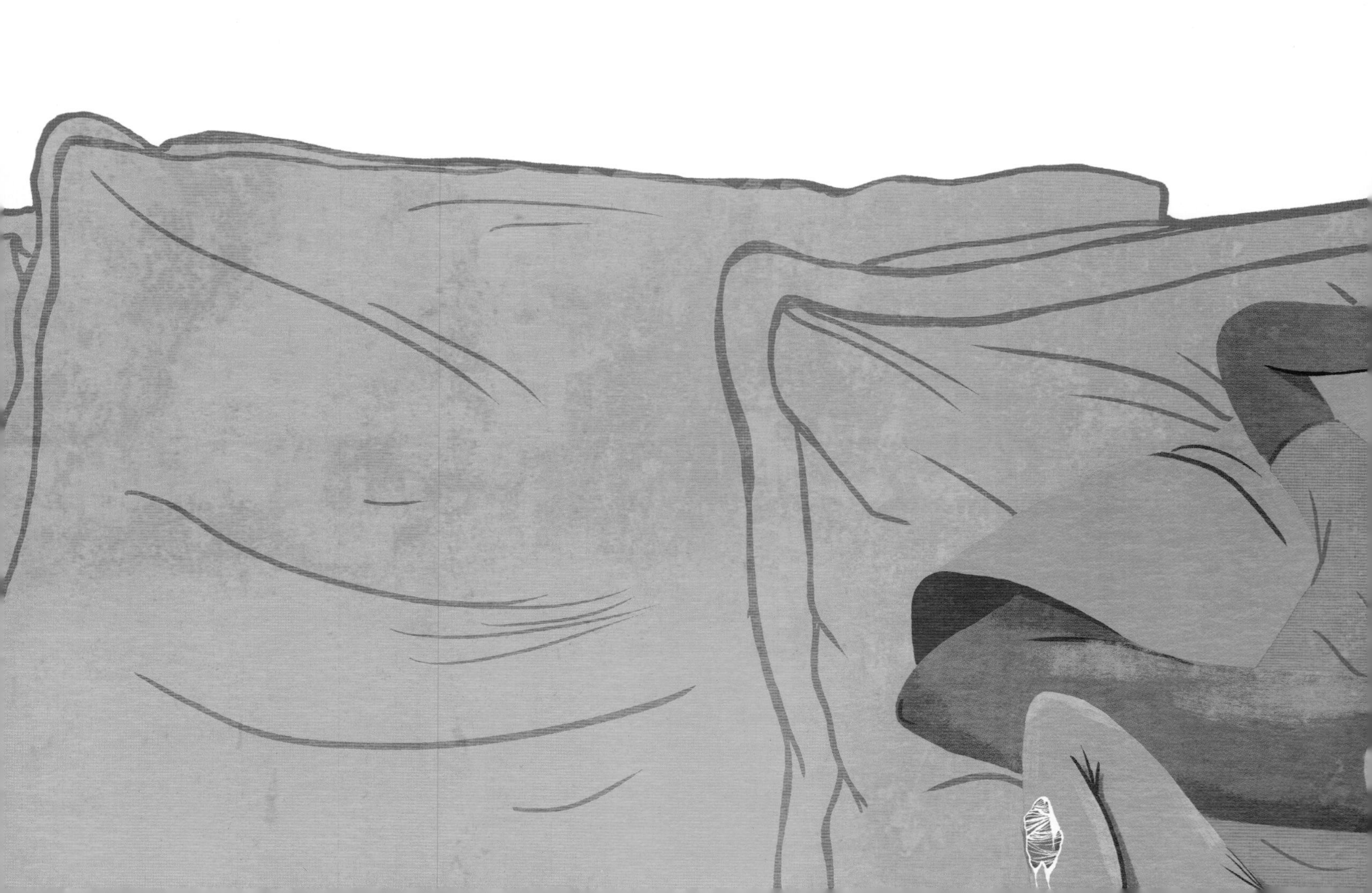

I hope you appreciate the extraordinary

even in the littlest things.

I hope you become a leader in rebuilding and nurturing the natural resources of our planet.

I hope you find your people—

people who love you and appreciate you for who you really are.

I hope you listen to others (even if their viewpoints differ from your own) and respect their beliefs

(even if you believe something else).

Appreciate that harmony exists when we all strive for balance.

I hope you find that no one puts you down
without your knowing how to pull yourself up.

I hope you live your truth
and experience every moment with an open heart.

I hope you learn how to help those who need a hand.

I hope you treat everyone with charity and kindness, showing mercy even to those who are mean.

I hope you know that you will always be

perfectly good enough, exactly as you are.

I wonder about the incredible journeys you'll take,
the amazing adventures you'll experience,
and all the beautiful memories you'll make.

And if you ever get lost, I am here.

I hope I have shown you the way. I know that you will learn more than I have taught you—and that you will, one day, come back and teach *me*. I know you will do more than I did. I know you will be amazing. I love you no matter what, kiddo, and you can always come to me and I will always listen.

Love,
Dad

Contributors

"I hope you don't let the world change your smile. Instead, let your smile change the world." —**Chase Mattson**

"I hope you shine a rainbow from your heart for all the world to see." —**Stephen McCarty**

"I hope you believe that superheroes exist in all colors, shapes, sizes, and genders—
and that most of them don't wear capes." —**Utkarsh Ambudkar**

"I hope you love your life and treasure every season along the way." —**Stevie Hendrix**

"I hope you always remember to choose happiness and the things that make you laugh." —**Matt Cohen**

"I hope you love big—and I hope the biggest love you have is for yourself." —**Andrew Gardner**

"I hope you know there is always something to be thankful for." —**Andrew East**

"I hope you have a life filled with dreams that come true!" —**Darin Brooks**

"I hope you feel love in every cell of your body, a boundless love that fills every day with happiness
and circulates back into the world around you." —**Robert Schwartzman**

"I hope you appreciate the extraordinary even in the littlest things." —**Brian Keys**

"I hope you become a leader in rebuilding and nurturing the natural resources of our planet." —**Eric Bilitch**

"I hope you find your people—people who love you and appreciate you for who you really are." —**Dan Bucatinsky**

"I hope you listen to others (even if their viewpoints differ from your own) and respect another's beliefs (even if you
believe something else). Appreciate that harmony exists when we all strive for balance." —**Joel Warsh**

"I hope you find that no one puts you down without your knowing how to pull yourself up." —**Chazz Lewis**

"I hope you live your truth and experience every moment with an open heart." —**David Elmo Cooper**

"I hope you learn how to help those who need a hand." —**Dan Payne**

"I hope you treat everyone with charity and kindness, showing mercy even to those who are mean." —**Mirthell Mitchell**

"I hope you know that you will always be perfectly good enough, exactly as you are." —**Christopher French**